D0130829

THE BALLAD OF BIDDY EARLY

For Eric and James – N.W.

For Paul Mariani – B.M.

Biddy Early

By Nancy Willard

Illustrated by Barry Moser

for my friend Maggie Chung ~ 5 August 1991

Alfred A. Knopf 🐕 New York

Library of Congress Cataloging-in-Publication Data
Willard, Nancy.
   The Ballad of Biddy Early / by Nancy
Willard ; illustrated by Barry Moser.
         p.   cm.
      Summary: A collection of poems
about Biddy Early, the wise woman of
Clare, and her animal, human, and
supernatural associates. ISBN *0-394-88414-0*
ISBN *0-394-98414-5 (lib. bdg.)   1. Early, Biddy,*
1798–1874—Juvenile poetry.   2. Children's
poetry, American.   [1. Early, Biddy, 1798–
1874—Poetry.   2. American
poetry]   I. Moser, Barry,
ill.   II. Title. PS3573.I444B35   *1989*
   811'.54—dc19   88-29187

There was an old woman
Lived under a hill,
And if she's not gone
She lives there still.

HOW I DISCOVERED BIDDY EARLY

I grew up in a family that loved cats, and we always got our cats from Mrs. O'Brien. Black cats, gray cats, calicos, cats the color of butterscotch — and Mrs. O'Brien's slim black tabby was the mother of them all. The tabby's name was Biddy Early.

"Named for a grand Irish lady," says Mrs. O'Brien, "and that's the truth. Biddy Early was born in 1798, and my father's people knew her. She was a great hand at helping folks."

"And how did she help them?" says I.

"With her wonderful blue bottle," says Mrs. O'Brien. " 'Twas small, like an iodine bottle, but she looked into it like a crystal ball, and people said she could read the future. She could cure anything. She never charged any money for doing it, either, and that's the truth. Oh, hers is a story worth telling. When you're grown, you can write it down."

If you go to Ireland, you will find that though Biddy died many years ago, people have not forgotten her. They still speak of the wonderful powers of Biddy Early, the wise woman of Clare.

In songs and poems, limericks and ballads, I give you the good lady herself, Biddy Early.

Nancy Willard
March 1989

THE BALLAD OF BIDDY EARLY

"I've an empty stomach,
you've an empty purse.
You feel your fingers freezing?
Outside it's ten times worse,
so listen to my story.
Forget the wind and rain.
It's time for bed," the tinker said,
"but pass the cup again.

"I sing of Biddy Early,
the wise woman of Clare.
Many's the man admires her
carrot-colored hair,
and many those that come to her
on horseback or by cart,
for she can heal a broken leg
or a broken heart.

"She keeps a magic bottle
in whose majestic eye
a tiny coffin twinkles
and if it sinks, you die.
It rises, you grow better
and slip out of your pain.
It's time for bed," the tinker said,
"but pass the cup again.

"She covers the great bottle
and runs to fetch the small,
filled with a bright elixir,
honey and sage and gall.
She'll take no gold or silver
but maybe a speckled hen.
It's time for bed," the tinker said.
"Let's pass the cup again.

"*Follow the stream,* she told me.
Go where the salmon goes.
Avoid mischievous bridges
for even water knows
if you should drop this bottle—"
He turned and spoke no more.
Biddy Early's shadow
was listening at the door.

HOW BIDDY PUT HER SHADOW IN ITS PLACE

Shadow, if you won't follow me
you shall follow the cat.
Let the cat follow the tree
and the tree follow the sky
and the sky follow the window
and the window follow the house
and the house follow the town
and the town follow the city
and the city follow the country
and the country follow the road,
the road I walk on, following you,
the walk I rise for in the morning,
the rise I climb for in the evening,
the climb I rest from at night,
resting my hands, my heart, my heels,
my heels where I lock you
without stitch or key.
With nightfall I lock you,
with footfall I lock you.
Follow me.

HOW THE MAGIC BOTTLE GAVE BIDDY ITS BLESSING

"Sighing stones, ghosts and bones,
and who will dig a grave
for roaring Tom, that bloody man
who with a pistol gave
death to seven people?
The gravediggers have fled.
So let the lightning bury him,"
the deathwatch beetle said.

"Even the wicked need a grave
and it's a dreadful thing
for any man to make his bed
under the vulture's wing.
Give me the spade and pickax.
A murderer who's dead
can do no harm to anyone,"
Biddy Early said.

She sank her spade into the sod—
the stones began to weep.
"The little mice," said Biddy,
"are singing in their sleep."
She sank her spade into the roots—
their cry turned her to ice.
The deathwatch beetle snickered,
"An owl has caught the mice."

Six feet down in darkness
she heard the shovel chime
against an old blue bottle
glittering under grime.
With sleeve and spit she polished it
and heard the bottle call,
"Of all things born at midnight
I am most magical.

"Nothing known shall come to pass,
no secret word or wish,
that I have not reflected.
Bird, beast, or fish,
every living thing shall praise
the healing in your hand,
Biddy, the bravest woman
in all of Ireland."

THE SPECKLED HEN'S MORNING SONG TO BIDDY EARLY

Let the speckled hens praise her.
Let the nine nations of slugs honor her.
Let the ten tribes of sparrows rejoice in her:

High-stepper, moon-catcher,
keeper of starlight in dark jars,
protector of pigs, saver of spiders.

Praise her from whom all cracked corn flows,
for whom the stars go willingly to roost,
for whom the gold loaf in the sky rises.

BIDDY REJOICES IN HER SEVEN-TOED CAT

I've pockets of starlight, so give me no money.
I've spells on each finger, I've no need of rings.
Though I'm plain as a plum, I am handsome as gold
when I fly through the woods on my queenfisher wings.

I've sixty sleek sparrows to carry my wishes,
my clock is a thistle, my servant a bee.
So pay me with goslings and roaring red roosters
and ponies and pigs, and I'll set them all free.

Take the tears of a toad if your sickness is simple,
touch the legs of a lark if your sickness is dire.
But by Merlin's best spell, I trust no one so well
as the seven-toed kitten that talks to my fire.

I've got an old cupboard that shows me the future,
I've got a gold thimble that calls down the rain.
Eleven lean shadows keep house in my rafters.
I call every one by its family name.

There's Doughface and Mothfoot and Tidy-Bones-Tiffany,
Babe-in-the-Bird-Down and Gristle-and-Grief.
There's Wink-in-the-Well and Starthistle-the-Dreamer,
and Timer-the-Rhymer and Timely-the-Thief.

The Captain-of-Carrots lives in the green bottle,
the Mistress-of-Mustard inhabits the red.
But at hearthstone and door, there's none I love more
than the seven-toed kitten asleep on my bed.

THE CAT'S FIRST SONG

There was an old woman of Coom
who kept a small ghost in her room
till her husband objected
to guests not expected
and was carried away by a broom.

HOW THE QUEEN OF THE GYPSIES MET TROUBLE-AND-PAIN

My name is Maureen, I'm the tinker-town queen.
My caravan travels from Gort to Kildare.
When my pony went lame, I remembered the fame
of Biddy the healer, wise woman of Clare.
Bright star of the morning, she gave me fair warning:
"Under my bridge huddles Trouble-and-Pain.
For the sake of this bottle, the creature will throttle
both you and your horse as you cross its domain."

I gave her a ring, hammered out like a wing,
I gave her green ribbons to tie up her hair,
a velveteen fan, and a new frying pan
and left with her blessing for Limerick Fair.
When we came to the bridge, my horse wouldn't budge.
The bottle grew frightened, it trembled and sighed,
and the harder I held it, the stronger I felt it:
a ghostly hand grappled, a ghostly mouth cried,

"May your horse never walk, may your son never talk.
May the saber-toothed gnats make a nest in your hair.
May your logs never burn, may your dog never learn,
and your purse turn to feathers at Limerick Fair.
May your buttermilk bark, may your lanterns go dark,
and your skillets and petticoats take to the air.
May you drown in the lake, unless I can take
that bottle of Biddy's, wise woman of Clare."

When it reared up its head, I took courage and said,
"By my mother's gold tooth and my father's glass eye—"
Then down the bridge clattered, the bottle was shattered,
but Trouble-and-Pain was more frightened than I.
Some say life is brief as the fall of a leaf,
and nothing lives long that lives under the sun,
but friends and relations in five gypsy nations
shall whisper my story till stories are done.

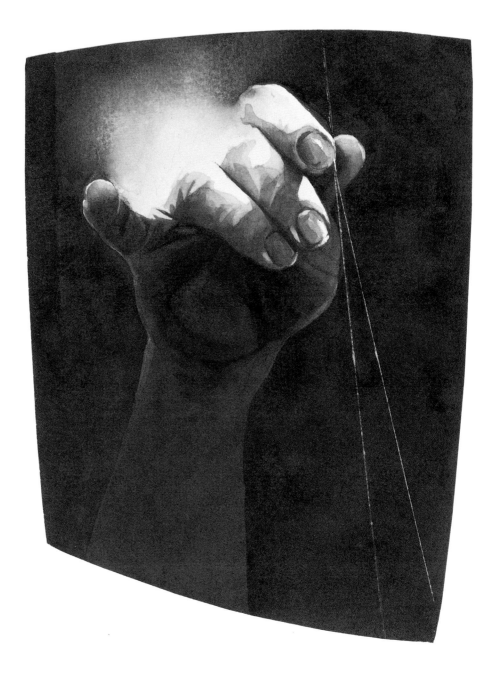

CHARM OF THE GOLD ROAD,

THE SILVER ROAD,

AND THE HIDDEN ROAD

On my thumb
I spun
two roads
from one thread,
half silver,
half gold.
I made them
and laid them
over the land
and said,

"May those who follow you
find gold but not glowworms,
coins but not crickets,
treasure but not tree toads,
silver but not silence,
money but not moonlight,
                  not magic,

              and not me."

HOW BIDDY HID MICK THE MOONLIGHTER'S
SLEEP IN HER SLEEVE

Mick came to her house at midnight
and pounded on Biddy's door.
"I have murdered William O'Sheehy
for sucking the blood from the poor.

"He put me out of my cottage,
he burned my house to the ground.
I have murdered William O'Sheehy
and will hang for it, if I am found."

Biddy spoke to her magic bottle,
she held it against her ear
and heard O'Sheehy's men riding
and whispered, "Go far from here.

"Take the little road to Liscanoor.
Speak to nobody on the way.
Take the broken dinghy to Kilrush
and a ship to Amerikay."

Mick wrote a name in the ashes
while the moon looked in at the door.
"Before I go, Biddy darling,
will you help me one time more?

"Will you tell the murdered man's sister
I'm wanted dead or alive,
and if she'll follow a wanted man
I'll send for her when I arrive?"

Biddy spoke to her magic bottle,
and the woods and the roads fell asleep,
the tinkers and turnips and mill wheels,
the soldiers and salmon and sheep.

Mick the Moonlighter's weariness left him.
It circled O'Sheehy's land
and darted through Biddy's window
and settled on Biddy's hand.

She folded its wings with a promise,
she stroked its breast with a sigh,
she made it a nest in her right sleeve
and closed its wicked green eye.

Not a soul stirred or wakened
from Feakle to Usher's Well.
O'Sheehy's men came in the morning,
saying, "Tell, tell."

"The bird has flown," said Biddy,
"where the moon and the stars run free.
The man you seek is fast asleep,
safe on the Irish Sea."

THE CAT'S SECOND SONG

There was an old woman of Clare
who was often seen riding a bear.
It ate candles and hay
till it twinkled away
down a tunnel of emerald air.

HOW BIDDY CALLED BACK FRIDAY,

HER LOST PIG

Friday, my lost pig, come and find me now.
May the thief that took you be a stone on Wednesday.
May the pen that keeps you be a road on Thursday.
May the rope that binds you run away on Friday.
On Friday, on Friday.
Day of the west wind on the nine fields,
Day to milk the eight cows of patience,
Day to crack the seven walnuts of wisdom,
Day to feed the six salmons of truth,
Day to bake you five loaves of bread,
Day to take your fear from the knife,
Day of acorns, day of sweet mud, day to open all gates
for my lost pig, my delight, my Friday.

A NOISY STORY OF HONOR AND GLORY

Honor the fox said to Glory the lark,
"The road to her house is delightfully dark.
I've brought her a basin for catching the moon
and five marrowbones in an old wooden spoon."

Glory the lark said to Honor the fox,
"I heard someone mutter. It rattles. It knocks.
It pads like a lion, it nods like a bear,
and it snapped at her messenger, Seed-in-the-Air."

Honor the fox said to Glory the lark,
"I hear Biddy's house is as broad as an ark,
with seven stars threshing their light for her bread,
and even the crickets are watered and fed."

Glory the lark said to Honor the fox,
"Oh, dinner most dreadful! Who nibbles and knocks?
You chatter of basins, the nightingale sings,
while someone is sampling the tips of my wings."

Biddy awoke. "Who has broken my sleep?
I heard someone mutter, I heard something weep.
It calls like a fox, it cries like a lark.
It has shaken the hush from my peaceable dark."

With her bottle locked up in its bullywood box,
she followed the sound of the lark and the fox.
"You may join my household and come to my feasts.
I dine with both earthly and heavenly beasts,

"the swan and the goat, the great bear and small,
the mouse in my kitchen—I've room for you all.
But Honor must promise what Glory shall sing:
Thou shalt not eat thy neighbor, nor nibble her wing."

BIDDY EARLY MAKES A LONG STORY SHORT

I, Biddy Early, come from the Red Hills.
My mother traveled under the cold sky
and carried me, her firstborn, on her back.
May the roads she walked stay with me till I die.

I am at home with hunger. For my bread
I learned to haul stones, scrub floors, and cook.
When Mother died, a wren taught me to read
the spells in streams and stones. Earth was my book.

The priest tells me, "Biddy, come to Mass."
I say, "Father, when I kneel down alone
the people whisper things. I want to live
out of their sight, with crickets and cats and stones,

"and when I die, I shall give back to Earth
all her gifts for the healing of hurts and ills.
I shall come back in water and words and leaves,
I, Biddy Early, asleep in the Red Hills."

HER FRIENDS REMEMBER BIDDY EARLY

"Who'll ring the bell?"
asked Wink-in-the-Well.

"The fox, the fox,"
said the new wooden box.

"Who'll say the prayer?"
asked Seed-in-the-Air.

"The priests, the priests,"
sang the heavenly beasts.

"Who'll carve her stone?"
asked the five marrowbones.

"The rain, the rain,"
sang the pig and the hen.

"Who'll give the blessing?"
asked the seven stars threshing.

"The moon, the moon,"
said the old wooden spoon.

"Who'll tell the story?"
sang Honor and Glory.

"I'll do that,"
said the seven-toed cat.

SONG FROM THE FAR SIDE OF SLEEP

Lullaby, my little cat,
Lord of Mouse and Knave of Bat.
Hail, Mischief, full of grace,
who did lately love this place.

Lullaby, your crescent claws
in the chambers of your paws,
which you sharpen day and night,
keeping all my kettles bright.

Lullaby, your gentle purr.
What small spirits did you lure
to the mushroom rings I made
and the lesser spells we laid?

Lullaby, your pebbled tongue.
Keep my velvets ever young.
Keep my slippers ever slick
with the patience of a lick.

Lullaby, your lively tail.
Never have I seen it fail,
spirits gone and revels done,
to point the quickest highway home.

Eternal life, eternal death
hang on our Creator's breath.
Little tiger in God's eye,
remember Biddy's lullaby.

NANCY WILLARD is the versatile author of many award-winning books for children and adults. She has written picture books, fantasy, poetry, short stories, essays, and adult novels. Her titles include *Firebrat,* a children's fantasy; the brilliant *A Visit to William Blake's Inn* (awarded the 1982 Newbery Medal); *Things Invisible to See* (honored as a Young Adult Best Book by the American Library Association); and *Water Walker,* a collection of poetry. She is a lecturer at Vassar College and an instructor at the Bread Loaf Writers' Conference, and lives in New York State with her husband and son.

BARRY MOSER has won numerous awards for his work, including the American Book Award for illustration, and his illustrations for *Jump Again!* received a *New York Times* Best Illustrated Children's Book award. He most recently illustrated *East of the Sun, West of the Moon* (a play based on the fairy tale), also by Nancy Willard, and the 1989 Newbery Honor Book *In the Beginning,* by Virginia Hamilton. He lives in New England.